The Peace Book

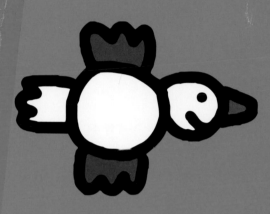

TODD PARR

Megan Tingley Books
LITTLE, BROWN AND COMPANY
New York ❧ Boston

ALSO BY TODD PARR:

A special note from Todd:

I remember in grade school being excited every year when I got my orange UNICEF box and went door to door collecting money. I always felt good that I was making a difference. Growing up in a small town in Wyoming, I never fully understood how big the world was or the impact one person can have on someone a world away. I'm proud that a portion of the proceeds from this book will help UNICEF spread its message of peace to the world.

Little, Brown and Company

Time Warner Book Group
1271 Avenue of the Americas, New York, NY 10020
Visit our Web site at www.lb-kids.com

First Edition

Library of Congress Cataloging-in-Publication Data

Parr, Todd.
  The peace book / by Todd Parr.—1st ed.
    p. cm.
  "Megan Tingley Books"
  Summary: Describes peace as making new friends, sharing a meal, feeling good about yourself, and more.
    ISBN 0-316-83531-5
    [1. Peace—Fiction.] I. Title.
PZ7.P2447Pe 2003
[E]—dc22
                                                                    2003058914

10 9 8 7 6 5 4 3 2 1

TWP

Printed in Singapore

Peace is making new friends

Peace is keeping the water blue
for all the fish

Peace is listening to different kinds of music

Peace is saying you're sorry when you hurt someone

Peace is helping your neighbor

Peace is reading all different kinds of books

Peace is thinking about someone you love

Peace is giving shoes to

someone who needs them

Peace is planting a tree

Peace is sharing a meal

Peace is wearing different clothes

Peace is watching it snow

Peace is keeping the streets clean

Peace is offering a hug
to a friend

Peace is everyone

having a home

DOG

Peace is growing a garden

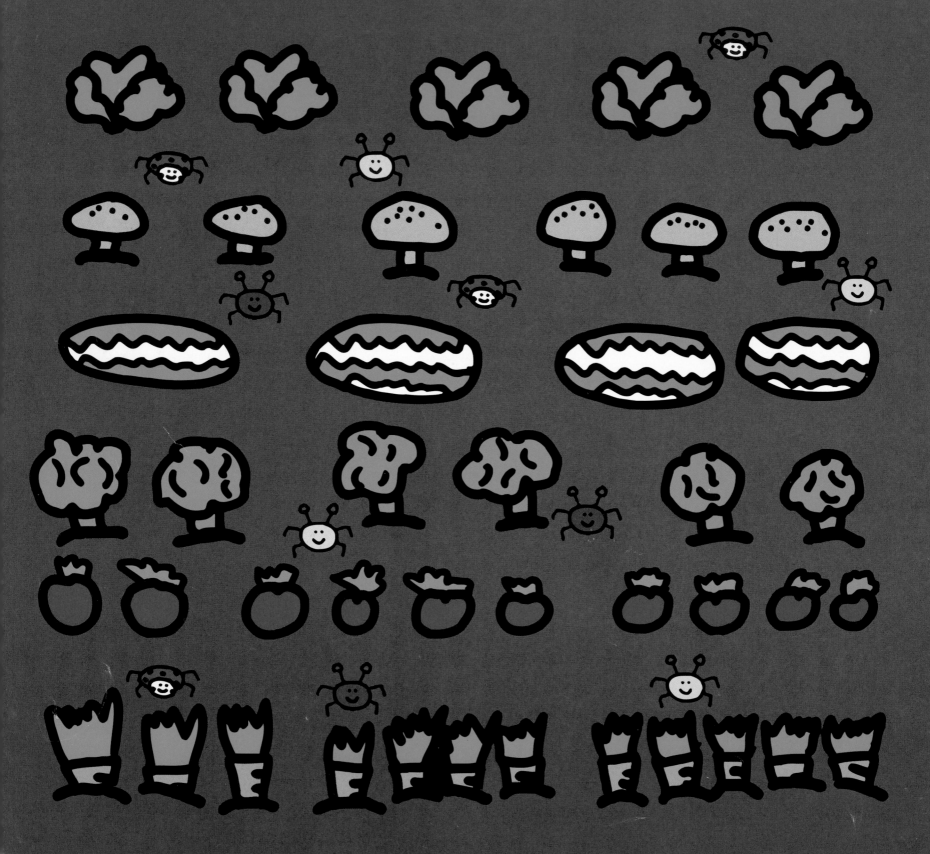

Peace is taking a nap

Peace is learning another language

KONNICHIWA

GURGLE

MEOW

GUTEN TAG

HOLA

Peace is having enough pizza in the world for everyone

Peace is keeping someone warm

Peace is new babies being born

Peace is being free

Peace is traveling to different places

Peace is wishing on a star

who you are

PEACE is being different, feeling good about yourself, and helping others. The world is a better place because of YOU!

Love,
Todd